This book belongs to:

. . . .

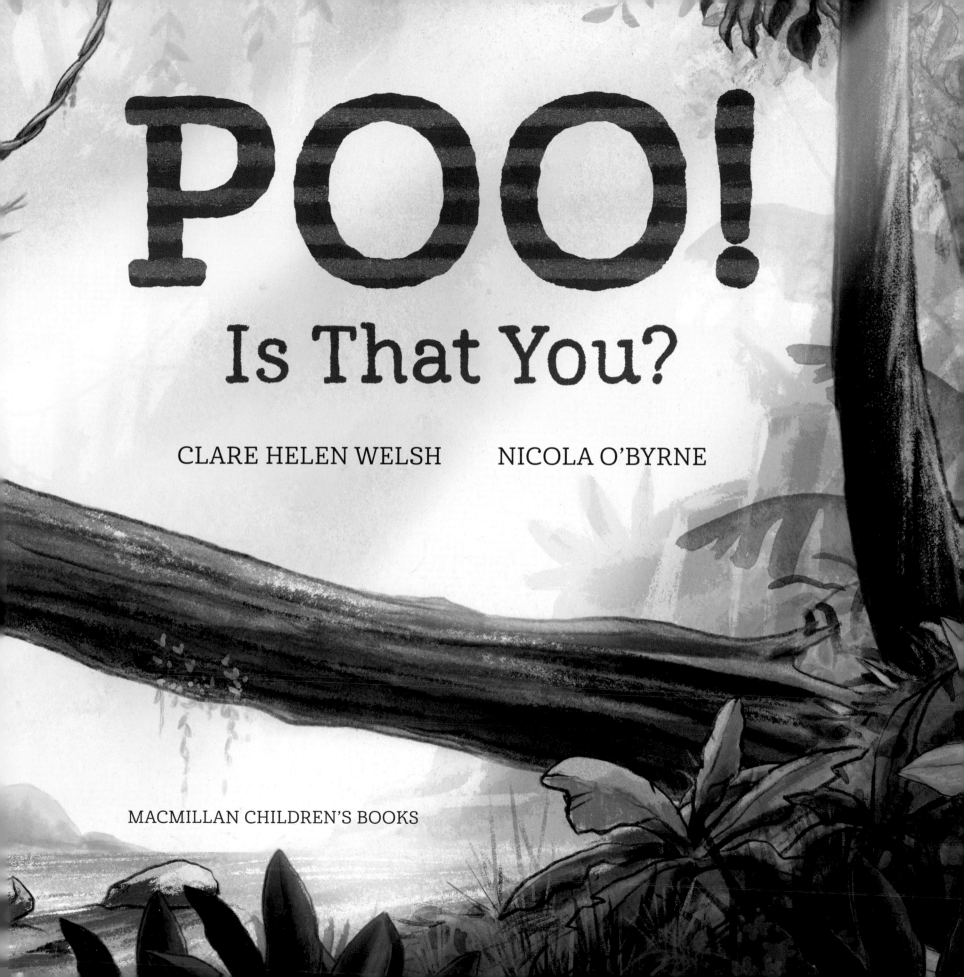

POO!

Is That You?

CLARE HELEN WELSH   NICOLA O'BYRNE

MACMILLAN CHILDREN'S BOOKS

Lenny the Lemur was on holiday in South America. He had found the perfect spot for a sunny, summer snooze when all of a sudden the wind picked up. A horrid, stinky smell wafted under his nose.

"PoOOOo! Is that you?"

He glared at a millipede crawling towards him.

"I don't think so," the millipede replied.
"But I do let out a stink when I get scared. Like this."
The millipede curled up into a spiral and squirted.

Lenny gave the squirt a sniff. It was definitely
disgusting. But it wasn't the **whiff** he could sniff.

Lenny closed his eyes and tried to put the smell out of his mind. But the **nasty niff** hung around.

"PoOOOo! Is that you?" he said to the stinkbird, nesting in the mangroves.

"Sorry," said the bird, a little embarrassed. "I do make a bit of a pong. It's all the leaves I eat."

Lenny gave the stinkbird a sniff. She was definitely pongy. But it still wasn't the **whiff** he could sniff.

There was a rustling in the grass ahead.

"Someone wants my sunny sleeping spot!"
thought Lenny, moving back into the sun
to continue his snooze.

But out ambled an anteater.

"**PoOOoo!** Is that you?" Lenny asked the anteater.
"Are *you* the horrid smell interrupting my snooze?"

"Maybe . . . possibly . . . I mean, I do stink.
But have you asked the skunk? He's way smellier than me."

"How rude!"
called the skunk,
who was playing in a hollow.

Lenny gave both the anteater *and* the skunk a big sniff.

But *neither* was the **whiff**
he could sniff.

He settled down in his sunny spot to try
and snooze, but it was no good.

Whatever it was, the **nasty niff**
was getting *right* up his nose.

"PoOOOO! Was that you?" he asked a tiny stink bug clinging to a leaf.

"Well, you did frighten me!" the stink bug replied, rather crossly. "And, well, that makes me smelly!"

But when Lenny sniffed the bug a second time, he realised it *still* wasn't the **whiff** he could sniff.

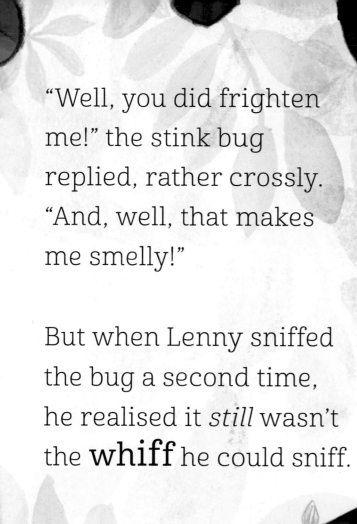

"I need some fresh air," Lenny said, holding his nose and climbing higher.

But up in the tree tops the smell
was stronger than ever.

"PoOOoO! It was you, wasn't it?!"
he said to a sloth, lounging in the branches.
"*You're* the **whiff** that I can sniff!"

The sloth wasn't bothered at all.
"I aa-am a lit-tle bit sme-ell-y . . ."
she replied slowly.

"I **knew it!**" said Lenny excitedly.
"It probably stops other animals
from eating you, doesn't it?
Like the skunk . . . ?"

"Not so, ac-tu-al-ly," said the sloth.

"You – see-ee, by the ti-ime I get cle-ean, I a-am al-read-y d-irt-ty aga-ain. That gree-eenish tinge you see on me is al-gae. And it can cause quite a stink."

"Yuck!" thought Lenny, but he wasn't interested in the details. He just wanted to sniff the sloth and nail the **nasty niff**. He took a deep breath and . . .

"Urgh! You do stink, but it's not you either!"
Lenny was completely fed up.

"Haa-ave you tri-ied the giii-ant peliiii-caan flower?"
said the sloth. She showed Lenny the way.

And eventually, a little time later, when they finally arrived, Lenny leaned over the plant and took a deep sniff.

It was *definitely* the worst thing he had smelt that day. But . . . the giant pelican flower was not the **whiff** he could sniff!

Poor Lenny's sunshine snooze was ruined.
The other animals gathered around him.

"What's the smell like?" asked the millipede.

"Maybe we can help," said the stinkbird.

"Well," sighed Lenny. "It's musty . . . and stuffy . . . and a little bit icky. And it seems to be hanging around me."

The millipede and the stinkbird took a deep breath, then looked at each other and giggled.

"PoOOOo!" they said.
"Lenny, it's YOU!"

"Me?" said Lenny.
"Me? It can't be!"

He carefully sniffed his
wrists and shoulders.
"Phew! So it is! It was
me all along!"

Happy that he'd found the source of the **nasty niff** at last, Lenny set off for his sunny, summer spot with a spring in his step.

Now that he knew it was his own **whiff** he could sniff . . .

. . . he didn't mind the **nasty niff** at all!

"WAIT!" called the stinkbird. "What do you use *your* smell for?"

"Watch this!"
said Lenny.

"**Finally!** Some peace and quiet!" said Lenny.

He settled down in the perfect spot for
a sunny, summer snooze when . . .
all of a sudden . . . the wind picked up.

A dirty, sweaty, cheesy **niff** wafted under his nose.

"PoOOoo!" he said.
"Is that . . .

. . . YOU?!"

SUPER STINKY FACTS!

Ring-tailed Lemurs use scent to mark their territory. They rub their tails on their scent glands until they're nice and smelly, then they wave them in the air. The stinkier the better.

Unlike most birds, the **Hoatzin** (or Stinkbird) mainly eats leaves. All this leaf-munching takes lots of digesting – resulting in a yucky poo-like smell! Salad, anyone?

Small but deadly, **Millipedes** can release a stinky poisonous spray. The spray from 100 giant millipedes is strong enough to kill a person. Eek!

If a **Lesser Anteater** feels threatened, it lets rip a smelly spray, five times stinkier than a skunk's – and that's saying something!

The **Skunk** has a very powerful weapon . . . stink clouds. With two stink squirters next to its bottom, fired by strong muscles, a skunk's aim is dangerously accurate.

Slow-moving **Sloths** are covered in algae. It's a bit smelly – but it makes the perfect home for all sorts of bugs. Over 900 beetles were once found on a single sloth.

There are over 5,000 different types of **Stink Bug**. But they have one thing in common – get too close and they'll spray a disgusting smelly liquid at you!

This enormous **Giant Pelican Flower** smells like rotting meat. An irresistible smell for the average fly . . . Yum!

DID YOU KNOW? You're one of the stinkiest creatures on the planet. Unlike most animals, **Humans** release smells from nearly every body part. If you didn't wash, you'd be pretty stinky!

For Harry and Evelyn – C.W.

For Penny, Becky, Josie, Sarah and Arabella – N.O'B.

First published 2020 by Macmillan Children's Books
an imprint of Pan Macmillan
The Smithson, 6 Briset Street, London, EC1M 5NR
Associated companies throughout the world
www.panmacmillan.com

ISBN: 978-1-5290-3047-1

9 8 7 6 5 4 3 2 1

A CIP catalogue record for this book is available from the British Library

Printed in China